UNBEATEN

STORIES UNTOLD

UNBEATEN

STORIES UNTOLD

C.J. Holiday

SBPC

SIMMS BOOKS PUBLISHING CORPORATION

SBPC

SIMMS BOOKS PUBLISHING CORP.

Publishers Since 2012

Published by Simms Books Publishing Corporation

Jonesboro, GA

Library of Congress Cataloging in Publication Data

2020925127

UNBEATEN: STORIES UNTOLD

ISBN: 978-1-949433-11-1

Printed in the United States of America

Book Arrangement by Simms Books Publishing

Editor Mary Hoekstra

Cover by Chester Hopper

All stories in this book are fictional, and are inspired by true stories.

I thought long and hard as I was writing this book, and how to talk about things that were out of my control. Getting it, all out has been part of my life, and now it's part of my healing. I wondered what the effects of my truth would be, what my truth would do, and how others, especially my parents, would take it.

I figured I could speak the truth and it would be fine, but most times, the truth is hard to digest. So, I've done my best to tell my story as well as I could, without intentionally hurting anyone's feelings.

I've spoken my truth here.

Chapter 1
"Humble Beginnings"

When my parents were born, the world was being torn apart by the racial wars in the American South and the North. Our country was adjusting to life, trying to bounce back from the Depression, then World War II was on the horizon.

The Great Depression did a number on all families and the United States as a whole. People lost everything they ever owned; others were restricted from working to make a fair living.

During the early 40's, the country was coming out of the Great Depression, and all the country's resources were being used to aide in the war effort for Great Britain. Imagine yourself running a store that sold silverware, and now you had to sell all your inventory to the United States military. Better yet, they turned your business into a plant to help make molds for plane parts and weapons.

Yes, this was happening all around the country, as the United States geared up for helping our allies in Europe in their war efforts, ultimately getting into the war fighting Hitler, then Japan. I say that to give you some background on the times when my parents were growing up and what would follow, the hardships, and them having to adjust and find their way in life at such young ages.

Midwest America was teeming with new employment and the rise of labor for military production. As mentioned earlier, there were race wars happening in the North and South; some whites rejected the need for, or help of blacks in the war effort. The country was at war and needed all hands-on deck, and that meant blacks also.

There were still the divisions by race, sex, and income during that time. Poor people stayed poor and had it hard no matter what color they were. The country needed labor, and they needed it "like yesterday," so most American families who were laborers really felt the hit; they got more work and less pay.

The country was in a state of conservatism, which meant conserving all of our raw materials for the war needs, and neglecting our people who worked hard day and night to supply those much-needed labor and materials. My family, on both sides, was affected during this time in history.

I can only imagine what it must have been like, growing up as a child, being poor, female, non-white, a non-landowner, and in an abusive family, too. I only mentioned these examples because if you were "all of the above" you were in the same boat. My parents' generation was all the ones affected by the fallout of history, prior to their births.

My parents' lives were similar in many ways; they both grew up without their biological mother, who had passed when they were young. My mom's mother passed when she was only three years old. My dad's mom died shortly after he turned 15 years old. So, as the above context explained, imagine growing up in a time when the country was in both a financial up-swing for the rich, and downswing for most poor laborers. That only worsened after the War.

Both my parents' fathers were left to either fend for the family or find another helpmate or family member to help out. Unfortunately, like most folks during that time, help was not there. Families were trying hard to keep the roofs over their own heads and could not be of much help.

My father's dad took the passing of his wife so terribly. With all the things going on in the outside world, he could not take another blow. Her death started a new chapter in his life. To his credit, he strived hard to maintain and raise nine children. My dad learned how to fend for himself, seeing examples from his father and older siblings; he became a responsible man at the age of 15.

Growing up without her mother, my mother was definitely a test for her father and her other siblings. From her earliest recollections, she remembers being taught how to be responsible, how to keep up a home, and the importance of family. Her grandmother stepped in to help raise her and her siblings. At the time she met my father, she was only 16 years old; he and she found some common ground.

My father had spent most of his young life as a latchkey child being raised by his older siblings, which was different, and learning to look out for himself. He had a head start, but a kid is a kid, no matter what situation they are in, and he was very mature for his age.

He found love and some type of stability with my mother. They were both young and shared the yearning for that type of love from another human being. They married at 16 and 18 years old. They had their first child, my brother, and shortly afterwards, they had me.

During the time when I was born, the world was again in shambles. My parents had to make do with what they had and do the best they could from the late 60's into the 80's. It was such a hard struggle for two young teens without proper guidance in life to parent two young children and raise them. Their value systems were built out of survival. That was the only thing they could pass down to their children, how to survive. This was not the only thing they passed down, but the cornerstone of our existence was to be survivors.

As I look back on how my parents were there for us, and how our childhoods had become all the things that were taught to us and most things that were not, I tell myself that they did the best they knew how.

Chapter 2

"A Mother's Burden"

I love my mother for all that she "showed" me, she was never a big talker but her actions spoke louder than words. I think about how people form their opinions, their ways of thinking and living, and it has a lot to do with what they have learned during the course of their lives. My mother had gone through a tremendous loss in her early life and was raised by her grandmother for a while. Naturally, a female child needs the nurturing of another female to help her grow and develop, so that was the best decision for her and her sisters. Her grandmother stressed the importance of family and other family values. After meeting my father, my mother and he moved away and started a family of their own.

My mother was brought up with a heavy presence of faith and going to church. She used her faith as her support system and her belief in the Scriptures reassured her that her young marriage was purposeful. She did her best to keep us in the mindset of keeping God first in our lives.

"We are the sum of our experiences"

Imagine this....

Born into an existence where your nurturer, creator in human form is no longer around. I'm sure somewhere in the human mind we know our mother, we feel her essence, it's familiar and part of us, so we feel that emptiness and void when she is no longer around. Despite growing up as a little girl with other female siblings and no mother, my mother's grandmother did the best she could to show her love. I think we all know the difference between what is right or wrong deep down in our souls, because what's right does not come with fear and unease, or pain and solitude, which we deal with in life.

My mother, I would say, was very protective over me, even somewhat strict. I remember that she would not want me to be alone around any older men, such as at church, or even boys my age. Would you blame her? Her experiences as a child and young adult prompted her protective behavior.

Chapter 3
"Daddy Knows Best"

Nowadays, you will hear people say, "There was no pamphlet or book that showed us how to be parents, we just learned and did what we could."

True for some... I think that the more you didn't know, you just winged it and prayed for the best, and some of us are lucky to have had the little that we did. After the death of his mother, my father was raised by his father and his other siblings. His father took the death of his wife and mother of his children very hard and started drinking more. You can imagine how hard it was for a sophomore in high school to navigate adulthood during a time in history when war was on the horizon, outwardly and inwardly.

Right after his mother passed, his father was grief stricken and had fallen into a state of depression. One day, his father left and never returned, leaving his nine children to care for themselves.

Talk about a double whammy! Losing their mother then their father in the same year took a huge toll on all of them. My father had sought work at the local gas station and then went on to work a night shift at the local drive through diner cleaning up the building after closing. He took care of himself and worked even three jobs at a time at some point.

His upbringing was not filled with riches or silver spoons but it was deeply rooted in love. His siblings banded together to make the best out of life as they played the cards that were dealt to them. They also had been taught good structure, faith, and the belief in God. His motivation in life was out of pure necessity, survival and he had faith to back him up. He learned that the world around him was just as harsh as the life he lived, and was fully equipped to deal with whatever came his way. Granted, he could only teach or share what he knew, and that was enough for him.

Chapter 4
"Pouring From an Empty Glass"

I know that my mom and dad did their best to show both my brother and myself all the love they had to give. You don't know what you don't know, and as teenage parents they knew enough to be dangerous. Overall, I can say that my childhood was a good one, but in retrospect, I guess it's all about what you perceive to be good.

Sibling rivalry had my brother and I going back and forth and rough-housing as kids. Back then, I always thought my brother was just being mean, but I guess that is normal when you have an older brother.

My father probably saw it as survival. Can you imagine being the youngest of 9? I'm sure he took a beating or two.

My parents had differences of opinion when it came to discipline and what constituted abuse. My father seemed to think the tougher you are, the better you can survive and live through anything; that was supported in how he had to fend for himself, so I get it. My mother saw it as cruel and unusual punishment; she and her siblings got along well and never really "rough housed," so she didn't see it as just innocent playing. She felt that my father maybe had some method to this madness, because my father turned out just fine and had become the man, she loved with all her heart. She was more prone to hugs and kisses, not push and shove. Even though it was child's play to me and my brother, it was still too rough for her liking. Safe to say, she held her breath each time we would roll around on the floor tussling, and my father would laugh as we would fight for the upper hand.

I just internalized it later in life that they could not give me more than what they had to give. I feel that not having a mother in both of their lives. The stepmother my mom had didn't treat her or her sisters right, so it ultimately affected how they were as parents. You can't give what you don't have.

Chapter 5
"Where is my childhood?"

When I think back, my childhood was mostly good, but the bad part of it would scar me for life. From as early as I can remember, I got a lot of attention. I don't know if it was the welcoming smile that I wore, my pretty, almond-shaped eyes, soft cheekbones, set of perfect baby blues, long blonde hair, but I was the center of attention. It never dawned on me that I was that focal point, I just loved being around my friends and doing fun things.

Growing up in a small neighborhood, in a small town, everyone knew each other, they knew about you and had met you, those were small town values, not to mention people are nosey. We played so many memorable games as children, we played "kick the can free," "I saw a ghost last night," and we rode our bikes endlessly into the night.

I remember our dad put in a swimming pool at our home and the company he worked for always had great gifts for us every year.

Our birthdays and holidays were very special. Hearing my mom play songs like "Frosty the Snowman," and my favorite was "I'm Getting Nothing for Christmas;" holidays made for great memories.

In my home, we were just like any other small-town American family, so I thought; we had good times and bad times, fighting with our siblings while our parents either sat back and laughed or punished everyone, no matter who started it.

Life in a small town had its ups and downs. I remember being a Girl Scout and loving it when it was time to sell cookies! I would sneak at least one box of my favorites to the side to eat later (those darn Thin Mints, they just kept calling me) I was busted one day by my troop leader. She wanted to do a count and we came up short a box of Thin Mints. I tried to hide the evidence, but it was too late.

She knelt down and asked me, "Breathe, I know someone knows about this missing box!"

I tried to hold my breath, turning bright red, I couldn't hold it anymore and I let out a breath and some cookies and chocolate followed behind. Ok, so what! I got caught red handed, but I was 6 and those cookies kept calling my name. You know what I'm talking about; they are so darn good!

Needless to say, I was no longer responsible for organizing, stacking, or even handling the cookies. I would just stand there, being pretty and calling folks over to buy our delicious Girls Scout Cookies. I know, it sounds like a great story, but no, my mom was our Brownie Leader and she was not going for that at all!

My mom worked at our school as a cook and an aide; she was always close by. You would think that having your mother at your school would have been a bad thing, but it was the best thing ever. I loved to see my mom walking through the halls of my school; being served lunch by my mother was wonderful.

My mom sold Avon, too. I took some and put the makeup on and she came to school that day and caught me with the makeup on.

School was not my favorite thing, to be honest, and having a learning disability did not help. I loved going out to play when I was younger, but I could not pay attention to what the teacher was saying during class. The recess time to socialize was the best part of school, holding court with all of my friends talking about whatever our young minds could think of. We would talk about what was on TV the night before, to what we ate for dinner, and what we wished we had for dinner. We were little children with great imaginations, wishing on a star.

I had all the confidence when I was around my friends, but somehow, I could not find my confidence when it was time for me to be in front of crowds. I remember my first play. When the curtains opened, I just froze, I could not remember the words of the song. Stage fright was something hard to get over, yet my friends knew me better when we had our time together, during recess at school. I redeemed myself when we did the *Wizard of Oz*, and I played Dorothy. I was even able to have my dog play Toro.

From kindergarten to sixth grade, I took dance classes. I was into Jazz and did acrobatics, also. I loved dancing; I even twirled the baton. I loved doing the different routines.

During church services, we would get in trouble for being a little too loud at times, but we were children with a lot of energy. My father and mother were deep into the church with family members on both sides who were church ministers. I spent most of my weekends in church, and Sunday school, and vacation bible school. We had a very strict home, so I was always a different child at home than at school.

I enjoyed meeting my friends at our weekly Brownies' meeting. We would do the same thing that we did at school during recess and talk about current events, who did what, and how they survived. Almost anything could get you in trouble; you could get punished for saying the wrong thing.

Our elders did not take too well to troublemakers; we were to follow what they said and not talk back. We were to just listen and be quiet young girls. There was always something about being a rebel. We didn't have that much to get us into too much trouble, except talking and carrying on were our ways of slight rebellion.

I would learn that the summer of my 11th birthday would change how I felt about being a rebel for the rest of my life, and change forever how I felt about being outspoken until I was made to feel ashamed to even speak at all. My friends and even my family would not know the toll what happened that summer took on my young mind, body and soul.

I remember my brother being sick a lot. He had an eye condition which required surgery and plenty of trips to the hospital. Living in a small town, we did not have all the resources of a big city, so my parents had to travel to the next big city to take him to a specialist. At times, when they took my brother to the city, I would have to stay with the nearest, or available family member or friend. So, I got used to being with someone other than my father and mother whenever they had to take my brother to see the specialist.

It has taken me four decades and more to revisit this part of my life... Here we go.

When I was 11, during a visit from my grandfather at our house, he molested me; that would take over my life forever. Your home is supposed to be your safe place. Home was where I was molested by my grandfather, my mom's dad. After it happened, I went and found my mom and told her what her dad had done to me. She told me to just stay away from him.

People always joked and blew off the things my grandpa did; they said it was all because he had a metal plate in his head, due to his injuries in the war.

I know my mom didn't tell my dad what Grandpa did to me, because if she had, my dad would have killed my grandfather. Needless to say, Grandparents Day at school was not a celebration for me. While other children at school shared the joy and love of their grandparents being there, I was hoping I never had to come in contact with mine again.

I tried for years to suppress what happened, thinking that I must have not experienced it at all. But it all came back to me, thinking about what happened, remembering I was abused in the worst way. How could someone touch a young girl like my grandpa touched me? How could he have touched me, who was his own blood?

I was so afraid to tell anyone; I didn't think they would believe me. Thank God it was an isolated incident. I knew my mom could sense that something was wrong, so she never took me back there again; I was relieved. I could not ever have gone through something like that again.

The times that my parents were not taking my brother to a specialist, and we were able to go on family trips, we went everywhere. We would travel to many places to visit family members. I enjoyed going to see my dad's brothers and sisters in California, which was one of my favorite places to go. My dad was the baby of nine and most of them lived in California. We visited Sea World, Magic Mountain, and the Wax Museum and we had a great time.

I remember spending time in Ohio at King's Island, a great water park and amusement park. For some strange reason, I remember I did not enjoy my time there, maybe because of all the long lines and miles upon miles of walking. Whew, no fun!

I would probably attribute it all to the trauma I had gone through that year. When you go through something like that, it really changes you. The next two years became a blur. It took time for me to adjust and really try to get back to some type of normal.

My brother's condition got worse; now it was his hips that gave him problems, so my parents were off to another specialist. This time, I was able to spend time with my aunts and cousins. I remember meeting them and my aunts were very nice to me, but my cousins were not. I guess, being close in age, you'll get that sometimes, but they were mean to me.

My aunt took great care of me. I had to spend a lot of time with them, even weeks at a time and sometimes more. I really enjoyed my time with my aunt during those young years.

I remember having a crush on one of my classmates. He was such a beautiful being, I loved everything about him. He knew that I was head over heels for him, but when I told my parents about him, they were against me having a crush or even dating. I thought that it was innocent, so one day I had him walk me home. When my father came home and saw him, he ran him away, he never came back. My parents sat me down and gave me the speech about little boys and dating, and it wasn't until I was 16 that I was able to date.

In middle school, I stayed busy with church or playing sports. I used to play softball and basketball and my dad was my coach for both of them. During the summer and school year I was cheerleader. I loved the school dances: as you know, I was a very good dancer.

Our town was very small and most of us knew each other or had seen each other before, so you would think that if anything happened it would spread like wildfire. My boyfriend I was with during middle school broke up with me, and that was my first heartbreak.

As I was a budding teenager, growing into womanhood, my body started to develop, from firmer legs from all of the sports and an even bigger breast size, so I'm sure I had admirers. One day, I was getting dressed in my room and didn't notice that someone was staring at me through my bedroom window. I turned around and saw two beady eyes staring at my half naked body! I screamed, ran out of my room, and my father ran out the house, trying to catch the perp! He did not catch him, but we always wondered if it was the neighbor from across the street. We could never identify him being the peeping-tom.

My high school years were great! With the exception of my younger years, I really didn't have anything else that was traumatic happen to me. I was adjusting quite well in life and tried my best to just drown out all the bad stuff with good times. I dated the high school quarterback. I stayed active in sports and cheerleading, which kept me real busy, plus there were weekends at church. I would say it was just like high school for most in a small town, where everybody knew who you were and the high school rivalries were classic.

I remember hearing all the wild things people would do to other schools, from stealing their mascots to TP-ing their school principals' house. I knew of a couple of friends who egged one of our rival schools and even stole one of the mascot costumes. It was one of the best times in my life.

I was also in beauty pageants. I was in Miss Niles, which I hated. My mom said that pageants would grow on me, but it never did, I won top five and top three. Right after high school, I went to beauty school and two years later I married my high school sweetheart.

Chapter 6
"A teenage love"

In high school I had a good time, I was the homecoming queen, cheerleader and popular. When my parents allowed me to date at 16 years old, that's when I met him, my childhood sweetheart. Now, I had known him just about all of my life, but when we decided to tell one another that we were interested in one another, that's when I met him for the first time. It was just like any teenage love, his coming to all the games to watch me cheer. Hanging out, going to the movies and out to eat. The nights on the phone were epic; we would sneak to be on the phone after hours when everyone in the house would be asleep. We would stay up for hours talking, and most of the time just breathing on the phone, waiting to see who would hang up first. I didn't know if I was in love with him at that point, or if I was just infatuated with him, or it was puppy love.

Time went by and even after high school we are together, and he popped the question. I was so happy to hear him say that he wanted to marry me and spend the rest of his life with me!

I had no reservations; I was convinced I wanted to spend the rest of my life with him and I knew that he felt the same way. We were engaged for a year and were in the planning stages of our wedding when I was told that my dad had stage four cancer. It was one of the worst days of my life; all I could do was think about it.

I was terrified that I could lose my father. I didn't know how much time we had with him, so I wanted to make sure that at least he would be able to walk his daughter down the aisle. As if I could handle any more bad news, my fiancé, the love of my life, my childhood sweetheart, broke more bad news to me. One day, he came to me crying and asked me to take off the ring. Now I was at a loss, wondering why he was crying, and how he could ask me to take off his ring. This was my forever ring, a symbol of our promise to each other to spend the rest of our lives together. After a long pause he went into telling me what was wrong. He explained that the husband of a lady he was working with was coming after him. He was not just coming after him, but that he had been cheating on me with the guy's wife. He gave me a sob story, saying that I deserved better and he wanted to call of the wedding three months before we were set to be married.

I loved him. I knew people made mistakes in their lives and forgiveness was necessary. I looked back on it later, and I should have never married him, because that was just the start of more bad things that would come between us.

I thought of my father, how proud he was of me, how he approved of him, and I did not want to break my father's heart. My father and mother had spent their hard-earned money to help pay for everything, and I could not let this one mistake ruin their or my happiness. Over 300 relatives were coming, so it was a big event. We got married. I forgave him. We had two children together. The road was not smooth at all; it was quite rocky at times.

I loved him and was certain that I could love him through anything. I'd spent years dealing with him, feeling unsupported by him. We were young, and he hadn't sowed his royal oats, and that pushed me to finally get a divorce. I could not take it anymore, plus it was having a bad effect on my children, so it was better for us to just be apart.

Now no one knew what was going on in our house. We'd had the fairytale wedding; he could do no wrong. I kept all the emotional abuse to myself. I didn't want anyone to know I was living in a failed marriage for all of those years.

Once you lose trust, everything else goes out the window. Conversely, if you can get away with murder, who will stop you from committing more crimes? No one. I prayed more than I had ever prayed up to that point, asking God to help make this man different, or release me from this marriage. Eventually, I was able to gain my reprieve. I looked back and knew I ignored the signs out of love, love and happiness, and I had to make sure I would not do it all again, just for love's sake.

Chapter 7
"Motherly Love"

To tell the truth, we were young, too young, and really had no idea what a marriage was all about. Yes, in the beginning it was a rocky road. At the tender age of 23, I had my first child. The excitement of having a little body coming to life inside my body, and the imminent fear of what I would do creeped in. I thought about what type of parent I would be. I had loved babysitting when I was younger, but having one of my own would be different. Not different in the amount of love that I could share with my baby, but different in that I would be responsible for this young life, for the rest of my life. Yes, it was a daunting task, but one I was ready for, and it was the happiest time in my life.

I was happy to have my child. I grew up playing with baby dolls and babysat all the time; I had a passion for children. My children had become my outlet and best friends, they would not judge and were always there listening and wanting to be around me, my children were very affectionate. This was something I had become so accustomed to that I did not even notice I was not getting the same affection from my husband. My husband showed his love in another way.

He was very helpful, he listened to all that was practical and made it happen. I went to beauty school and planned on running my own business one day, and he surprised me by building my shop in our basement.

There was more responsibility once the children were born. We never fought about anything, but he was a liar. We were so young and he seemed so depressed all the time, it felt like he was trapped. The lack of communication in our relationship did a number on us. Even though it was a short marriage of about six years, I divorced him shortly after.

Our life was pretty calm. He was good to me. He got remarried, but called me before he was about to get married and told me if I would have taken him back, he would have stood her up at the altar. I think sometimes, if I would have taken him back, how my life would be. After he was married, his and my children's relationship suffered. They did not see each other for four years. His new wife and I did not get along and she wanted to take my children away from me. I did a lot to help her, but in the end, being good to her backfired.

Chapter 8
"Sleeping with the Enemy"

I took some time to myself, and by time I meant, a long time! I was by myself, not dating or anything for six long years, just taking care of my children and going out from time to time. My girlfriend started dating a guy and she was always trying to get me hooked up with someone. She would not give up, until one day, I said "Okay, I will meet this guy." She introduced us and he was a nice-looking guy but a bit younger than I was. I did not recognize him at all, but he said he had gone to the same school we graduated from. I never heard anything bad about him, I just didn't know him.

We started hanging out more and I was getting to know him. There were some things I liked and others I did not. We started partying more often, and I was not a drinker at all. I was something of a light weight, so I tried to keep my drinking to a minimum, but after three weeks of hanging out, I started drinking more.

I didn't think it was a problem at that point, but then I had to check myself. I didn't want my children to suffer from my drinking getting out of hand or anything bad that could come from it, so I had my boundaries and no-nos. I noticed one day at a party, I saw him smoking and it was weed, and I didn't like it at all. We had several arguments about his weed smoking and he promised he would not do it anymore, and not in my house.

All of his promises had been empty, because one day when I came back home, his friends were there and he was smoking weed. We had a big argument and I told him this was not working out and he had to leave. He begged me to forgive him again; he said he was planning on marrying me, but he had only known me for about six weeks. That was his way of trying to sweettalk me into staying with him. He was a great actor and manipulator. Everyone who knew him had great things to say about him, but behind closed doors I knew better. Against my better judgement. I forgave again and we stayed together, but not without daily and weekly drama. I was dealing with a person who could tell me a lie with a straight face, convince me he was not lying, and that he loved me and only me.

Again, I took him back and I didn't notice it at the time but I had taken on a lot of his characteristics; drinking and smoking had become the norm and I was losing myself every day. There was a problem that came up with a child support check that came from my children's father. We were really struggling at that point, taking a step back, and thinking about that moment in my life, I could recollect just how bad it had become. I was so absorbed in doing everything that my man was doing that I lost my total identity and was in danger of losing all I had worked for and loved.

I had spoken to my parents about the missing check. I told them I felt someone had stolen it, and that someone was him. I knew my previous marriage was a failure and they wanted nothing but the best for me, so they were very critical of the new boyfriend. You know, sometimes what it looks like, it is, and I didn't have the heart to tell them what they were already thinking. I did some research and found out that the check had been cashed in a city over from where he stayed. I didn't have solid, concrete evidence that it was him, because I didn't catch him red-handed at that time, but I knew in my heart he did it.

I knew he had it and when I confronted him about it, he denied it. Of course, my mom and dad were really mad at me, and he and I got into it, you know, and started arguing about it. He said,

"You're not going to get rid of me and we're going to work this thing out."

He threatened that he would hurt my mom and father. Knowing my father was not in his best health, that scared me to death. By then, he had taken total control over me, which affected all aspects of my life, down to not visiting my parents as much as I used to do. It took a toll on my relationship with my family and friends.

At some point, my father expressed how he felt with me and threatened to tell my children's father about what was going on, and that he should get full custody of my children. I wanted so bad to tell my father what was really going on but feared for his safety. My father saw what was going on with me. He stressed to me that I didn't need to be around this guy anymore, and to make a decision between him and my family and children. My boyfriend had other plans and he was planning on doing something that would change my life forever.

Weeks had gone by, and still we were at odds. I could not leave him and he was not gonna let me leave without hurting someone. He had planned a trip to Las Vegas. He told me we had some stuff that we were supposed to get done. I had sent my children over to their father's house that day because it was his scheduled weekend, and when I got back, we started arguing. I can't remember the rest.

I felt really drowsy when I woke up, not knowing where I was or how I got there. The last I remembered was the argument we just had. Dazed and confused, I looked out the window and could see city lights and buildings from my seat on the plane. It was night time and all the bright lights woke me up; I struggled to get my bearings and understand what was going on. I remembered not seeing anyone else once I came to, and we were at a hotel looking out over the city. I wondered, *What the heck is going on?*

The next thing that happened was that he was sitting across from me in a chair while I was sitting on a bed. He said to me, "So now that we are here, I want you to tell me that you don't want to be with me."

I was too scared to say anything, I didn't know if I said the wrong thing that he would kill me or not. Besides, no one knew where I was and I had no clue of our exact location. I had him thinking everything was okay, that I wanted to stay with him, because I was afraid he was going to kill me. I didn't know what he was going to do with me. He would leave me in the room, and be gone for hours at a time while we were there. By this time, we had only been there a couple days.

The first chance I got, when he was gone, I went down to the pool. I didn't have a key, so I knew I wasn't going to be able to get back in. I saw a lady sitting out at the pool and I ran down there and I told her,

"Listen, I know it sounds crazy, but I've been kidnapped. I don't want to be here with this guy. Can you please help me? I'm scared. Can you call the police?"

I'm sure she thought I was crazy. But I told her, "Please, I need help."

She said, "Let me go get my husband," and as she got up and started walking away, the so-called person, my soon-to-be ex-boyfriend, came down to the pool and went inside. I don't remember anything else.

I remember walking down the streets in Las Vegas, I was wanting anyone to help or save me. He reminds me,

"Nobody will save you, they all look at you, but nobody looks at you like I've looked at you, you are my girl."

I do remember, when we were in the hotel room, I heard the back of the toilet lid being lifted off and put back on; when I went in there when he was out of the room, I looked and there was a bottle in the tank that looked like alcohol. I didn't really see what was in it, though. There was a refrigerator in the room, so I don't know why he'd be keeping alcohol in there.

Something was up, he must have drugged me. I don't remember. I don't remember getting on a plane again at all and I vaguely remembered the car ride from Chicago.

I called the police and told them what happened. They asked, "Did you go on your free will?" I said, "I don't remember." I thought about it initially when he had bought the tickets. We were dating only about two or three weeks and, initially I told him I would go. I made a report. I called and told him that we were breaking up for good this time. I was not gonna change my mind. I had enough.

I was really ready to start my life over again and be free of him for good. I went out with my girlfriend and her husband one night, taking some time to relax and have some fun. My mom's friend asked to borrow my car; she was trying to see if her husband was cheating and she wanted to follow him without him knowing. I left her the keys to my car and to hang out with my friends. I left her a message, that when she dropped of the car to leave my keys in my mailbox.

So, I went out with my girlfriend and her husband. We got home about two o'clock in the morning and my car was in the driveway, but my keys were not in the mailbox. So, we stood out there in the cold, thinking how the heck am I going to get in. And why wouldn't she leave my keys?

So, I was just standing there and all of a sudden, he kicks the storm door off the hinges. I'm there with my girlfriend and her husband; he is yelling at him like I was with him. He had my keys and used them to get into my house. He must have been watching my house when my mom's friend dropped the keys off in the mailbox. He was calling me all types of whores. I tried to calm him down. My friends wanted to stay and suggested I call the police. I told them it was alright, they could go. I didn't want to tell her yes, because I didn't know what he was going to do to me.

After they left, we were inside and I remember it being real dark, he kicked me in the small of my back and I fell to the floor. He ran to the door and used the keys to lock all of the deadbolt locks on the door, then put the keys in his pocket. He pulled all of the phone cords out of the wall and started getting real belligerent. Every time I got up, he just kept kicking me back down. I went and tried to sit in the window seat after about three or four hours. My body was banged up; not having any carpet on the floor did nothing to break my fall. I was sitting in the window seat and he grabbed my feet and pulled me out by my feet. I thought I broke both my wrists and my tailbone, so I started crying. He went over, picked up the loveseat, and threw it like he was Superman. A friend, years later, told me he was on acid.

He threw the loveseat and it hit the wall. He broke a beer bottle open and said he was going to cut me open with it, but he didn't; he ended up cutting himself. He didn't sleep for close to a day and a half. Finally, he went to sleep Sunday morning.

I knew that my kids were gonna be coming home that afternoon. I told myself I could not have my kids in the house like this. I was so scared that nobody would look for me because it was the weekend. I didn't have the kids, so I didn't have anybody stopping by. So I was praying somebody would please stop by.

The next morning about 10 o'clock, I went downstairs and he had fallen asleep on the floor. I reached in his pocket and my keys were there. I was so scared he would wake up. I had tears coming down my face and didn't want the tears to fall on him while he was sleeping, so I made sure to wipe my face clean. I didn't know what I was going to do, if he was going to grab my hand, or kill me, as I was reaching for the keys.

I grabbed the keys. I let myself out. I ran outside. I went to the neighbors and I called my girlfriend and had her come by. She took me down to the police station so they could see that I was bloody and beat up and do a report. They told me I had to serve him an eviction notice to get him out. I said he didn't even live with me, so they sent a car out, and I came home, and he was gone. He wasn't at his parent's house; they couldn't find him.

So, weeks would go by. He would do stuff like cut my kids' swing down at my mom and dad's house and he would go through their glove box and other things. And at this time, my mom and dad were not even talking to me, because they thought I had taken him back; they didn't know that I was just trying to keep him away from them because he had said he was going to hurt them. Knowing how much he hurt me, I thought he was really going to hurt them.

He was stalking my children and me. His parents lived across the street from where my children went to school. He would call and tell me what my daughter was wearing that day, what my son did at recess. He would wait for five weeks, sometimes three or four months, and would randomly show up at my beauty shop. He would just come in. So, of course, I didn't want to call the cops because I didn't want to lose my customers, but then he would leave.

I was scared. On the weekends, when I didn't have my children with me, I would ride around with the cops looking for him or I would go to my girlfriend's house. One weekend, I went down to my girlfriend's house, and when I got to her house, her phone started ringing. It was him. He called and left a message on her answering machine, probably 30 or 40 of them, saying, "I know where you are and I'll come get you and you are a whore."

We didn't know if he was gonna actually come down to her house, so we were pretty scared. We left and went back to my house. We checked around the street for cars and signs of him, but didn't see anything. Once we got back into my house, we hurried and locked the doors.

We slept in the same room together and heard a noise, which sounded like someone was walking down the hall. We could hear the footsteps coming closer.

"Oh my God!" I said, "It's him!"

He was hiding in there. I bet he didn't even go anywhere, just camped out at my house. I think he just said it hoping we would come back there or that I was with someone. When he came down the hall and he flipped the light on, he saw me and my friend. I don't know if he was relieved because he thought he would see another man, but he started cussing and calling us whores and all kinds of other names. He didn't actually do anything to us that night. He laughed and left, and I called the police like I always did.

I thought he'd found a girlfriend or something, because he wouldn't bother me for a while, about nine months to a year later.

When we were together, earlier on in the relationship, he bought my kids a dog. When he left, he took the dog with him to punish me and the kids, so he left a message on the answering machine:

"I'm leaving town. You don't have to worry about me again. I'm really sorry for everything I've done. I've been taking drugs and I normally wouldn't do this stuff and I can't take the dog with me where I'm going. So, if you don't mind, I can leave the dog in the beauty shop. You don't have to be in there. I know the kids will be so happy to have the dog."

When we started dating, he wasn't on the hard drugs, he just drank and smoked weed. He was a very nice man. Something just went wrong.

I had my friend Scott staying with me and the kids; he was a deputy sheriff and made me feel a whole lot better when he was around. He was sleeping on my couch.

My ex would never come bother me when he knew that my kids were home. He called and said he was coming to drop off the dog. I noticed a car pull up and then drive away, I thought to myself that he had just dropped the dog off and left. I went down to the beauty shop to check. I couldn't see because it was pitch dark out there. I didn't see who got out of the car because the light switch in the beauty shop was all the way across the room. I had to walk to the other side to cut the light on. And then I remember hearing the beauty shop door shut. So, I rushed down the steps. I thought about the kids being so happy that the dog was back.

I took two steps down there, down into the beauty shop. There was no dog, and he was standing in there. He'd had somebody come and drop him off and then leave.

Then he attacked me and raped me. He pulled my hair and I was trying not to make any noise because my kids were home and my friend was right there on the couch. I had no idea that he was gonna rape me; I thought he was just there to beat me up. My friend could have come and helped me, but being raped is not something you want the kids seeing. I didn't really understand. I don't know if there's a power thing because he didn't actually ejaculate, he just put it in, being really mean, pulling my hair, and he was just doing it just to do it. Then he left.

I didn't hear from him in six to seven months, something like that, and I had started dating somebody. I told him the reason I had all the deadbolts on my doors and the reason I had my windows nailed shut. I explained and told him that somebody I used to date still bothered me every once in a while, and he had done some really crazy stuff. I never went into much detail.

The cops could never get him, because we lived really close to the Michigan/Indiana line. And so, when he would do something, he would just go really quick over to Indiana and they couldn't get him. So, the cops actually put us in a safe house in Tennessee. The cops drove by looking for him and did not find him.

He left a message on my answering machine and said, "You're such a dumb bitch and these cops are dumbasses."

He said he sat in my house, on my bed, looking out the window, watching the cops drive by repeatedly, day after day, looking for him. He tormented me, and all I could do was cry. I called the police and made another report. I told them he was in my house all along while they were looking for him. Three or four months went by after that, and I heard nothing from him.

I had a Thanksgiving party for all my friends and I had started to date a guy. He stayed at my house quite a bit. He would stay when my friend's other friends couldn't stay, because we were never by ourselves.

His cousin was coming into town. He asked me if he could go back to his apartment because he really didn't want us to be there when his cousin came into town. He said he didn't want them to be around us. I agreed. Nothing had happened for a long while, no calls, so I thought the coast was clear and we were good.

So all my friends had left about six or seven cars in the driveway. They pulled away, I turned off the lights in living room, walked the kids into the bedroom both my two kids shared, tucked them in bed, and started walking down the hall. I got ready to take off my pants and put on pajamas, and as I was bending down, somebody banged really loud on my front door.

I was thinking, *why is he banging so loud?* My friend that's a cop was kind of obnoxious sometimes, so I was thinking, *he knows I just put the kids to bed.* It took me a while to get to the door because I was putting my pants on again. I'm so thankful it took me sometime, because I would have answered the door and been attacked by my boyfriend.

As soon as I got to the front door, I heard glass breaking. It was him! I ran around to my kids' bedroom window, looked out, but there was no car in the driveway. That's why I knew it was him; he would always park one street over and then come around. I ran down the hall and he come around to my bedroom window and started busting it out. I called my mom and dad because they lived a block away. On the phone, my dad could hear the glass breaking in my bedroom and him yelling,

"You whore! Ima kill you this time!"

My dad could get there a lot quicker than the police, so my dad called 911 and then headed over to my house. There was a lot of snow out there, and my dad, having stage four cancer, did his best to walk through the snow and get to me. He was really weak and had slippers on but one had fallen off, and my dad was trying his best to catch him.

My dad told me he had parked his car in my neighbor's driveway; that's why I couldn't see his car.

Thank God my dad was there to run him off, he called and made a police report that day. Before we knew it, I had a lawn full of police cars, from state police to local police.

Many of my friends would stay with us from time to time and nothing happened for about four months. Then, one day we found one of our dogs was hung on the clothesline when we came home. That was his way of letting us know he was still around.

It was mid-February and my girlfriend called and asked me if I was sitting down. I sat down and told her, "I am now." She asked me if I had read the paper; it was Sunday and I hadn't read the paper just yet.

She said, "You need to, because a certain person has died. I asked her to clarify, "Are you sure, because he was only 28 years old."

I busted out the door and ran to go get a paper. My mom and dad were at my house that day and I cried all the way back home. When I got back home, I took all the nails out of my windows and finally, I could breathe.

I was free! I didn't have to live in fear and hell anymore. I still couldn't believe it, but it was true; after three years of being tormented, it was finally over. A week went by and I got a letter from his parents. They lived not too far from me, across from the kids' school. They left the eulogy in my mailbox. On looking at it, I noticed they had circled "You were not there." I didn't know what to make of it.

I feel like I've never found closure on this. I didn't know he was sick. This scared me so deeply; I don't know if they even knew just how much grief their son had caused me. I prayed about it and started on my journey toward trying to live a normal life.

Chapter 9
"Shellshocked"

Let's see, new normal...*hmmm what is that anyway?* I had just gone through three years of pure hell, suffering both physical and mental abuse, almost losing my relationship with my parents, my sanity, and my life. I thought, *we shall see how this goes.*

I am forever grateful that my children were protected, in the sense that they did not get physically harmed during all of this craziness. I remembered always having them on my mind through it all; I could never have forgiven myself if something had happened to them.

I figured I'd take the blame for most of what happened and wondered, *could it be my fault to begin with and did I try hard enough?* I wrestled with these thoughts every waking moment. *Did I do enough to stop it?* I believe that I did in the beginning, with telling the police about what was going on, but they just could not catch this lunatic. I had let him get away... not yelling out when he was raping me in my salon, knowing that I had help right upstairs with my friend who was a police officer sleeping on my couch; he could have ended this that day.

I had nightmares about holding a gun and shooting him before he attacked me. I could not bring myself to do such a thing; in the back of my mind, I thought about getting in trouble and going to jail, because I could not prove that he was abusing me and no one was there to catch him in the act. Feeling like my hands were tied, I felt hopeless, shameful, and dirty. Battling between the thoughts, *I could have ended*

43

this, and *Why didn't someone help me?* had burden my mind. I tried to put it out of my mind when I found out he had passed, trying to find some joy in it, and being relieved it would never happen again. But I am still and forever reminded that it happened. *What do I do now?*

They say life goes on...right? How do we just magically get up, dust ourselves off, and move on with life, especially when you are made to feel all alone in this journey? Yes, I say "made to feel all alone" because at certain points of that three-year campaign of hell, no one really understood, or they just pointed the finger and offered no real solution. I was trapped, so anything other than taking him out sounded like words of damnation of my character and being in defense of him.

I tossed and turned in my sleep one night, waking up in a pool of blood, I could feel both hot and cold spots on my bed beneath me. I reached down to feel around, trying to locate where it was coming from, reaching under me and around my neck, chest and legs. It was so much I could swim in it. I jumped up and ran to the bathroom and to the shower. I could not find any cuts on me and from my recollection I was not on my period at all. I washed myself with steaming hot water and soap. After my shower was done, I could still see the trail of blood leading back to my bed. I took a step toward my bed and then lost my footing and fell back into the pool of blood, face down, struggling to get out of the bed, literally drowning. Gasping for air I found myself grabbing for the side of the bed, only to end up with blood-soaked sheets as I sank deeper into the mattress. I was suffocating. I let out a loud scream, fearing I was about to die. Then I woke up.

I sat on the edge of the bed and screamed as loud and as hard as I could into my pillow, as the tears wet my pillow and my mascara stained the pillowcase. That was just one nightmare; my self-accusing spirit would not let me sleep a restful night. I felt like I could have done something, yelled a little louder, fought back to save my life.

Looking at the woman in the mirror, I did not recognize her, she was someone I'd never met before. I was scared, yes, even scared of my own shadow. The thoughts of him lived in my mind for three years, and I was just hoping he would not be around the next corner, steal me away again, and take my life. This new person was beaten down, insecure, nervous, counting every second and minute of the day when I could free myself of this horror.

I prayed. I spoke about it, but the dreams, thoughts and nightmares would not go away. I can say that I developed PTSD and was just like a solider who came back from experiencing combat. It was unnerving and unsettling. Life is flipped upside down.

I tried to get myself some help for this, but it seemed like it did not work. I was told, because of the amount of time I experienced this trauma, that it could last a lifetime. Or it could be as little as six years before I could put it in the right perspective and have a whole, full life again. I fought with the feeling that even in death he was haunting me from the grave. I had gotten into such a routine of fear, hiding, holding my breath, not knowing what was around the corner, or if he was there to attack me. I really had to work on the fear and also on the self-hating issue I was having. I just could not forgive myself for allowing this to happen. Being told, "It's not your fault," took me back to instances when I could have done something. This plagued me. I kept trying to rationalize it, speaking my truth and getting comfortable in knowing that I did what I had to do and that was enough.

The emotional and physical scars won't go away. It's just I have to find a new way of dealing with them and making sure that I have a healthy mindset to be able to see the signs before it ever gets to this stage again.

You really never know what folks are thinking, let alone what they are capable of doing; you just have to have your antennae up.

Sometimes, questioning the "why" may never give you the answer. I always wondered if it had been something about me. *Did I miss something, or allow certain things to happen because of my upbringing?* This had me on an emotional roller coaster, trying to figure it all out. In the end, I figured you just have some crazy people in the world, and no matter what you are for or against, they have their own motives in mind. He was greedy with power and control; he wanted to control me and make me his prisoner.

Now I am free from him, realizing he can no longer just pop up and abuse me, make threats, and show that he could reach out and hurt someone I love at any moment. He was gone. I should be alright now. I should be about moving on with my life. This period in my life had etched permanent fear in my brain; it had become automatic and I looked for him to jump out at any time. Months had gone by and I was still trying to adjust to my new normal. I kept to a safety routine pretty much everywhere I would go and especially at home.

I lived in a nice-sized home, which sat a good distance away from the road. It had two levels, the living level upstairs and the shop downstairs. From my previous three years of hell, I would do safety checks each time I came home. Driving down the street I would make sure I saw any familiar cars or things that would stick out as unusual, sometimes even driving my street twice before going into the house. Once at home, I made sure I could get into the house without anything stopping me, so I would purposely leave my doors open so I could get right in.

I know, not really a smart move, because I knew it was not gonna be him stalking me anymore, but someone else could have had easy access to my home. Still, I was so used to the encounters I experienced with him that I could not risk trying to find my keys to get into my house, so I needed immediate access. My fear had me absolutely petrified from the car to the house. Having this feeling somebody's going to come and get me still is something I deal with even today. So, it's weird. It's like somebody can be sitting in my house, but I guess I'd rather have them in there, because then I'd get the chance to run out, just in case.

I currently live in a little apartment and feel petrified to be in a big house all by myself. This is perfect for me; I can see everything in my place all at once with the exception of my bathroom and bedroom. I have gotten a little better in being more comfortable in my space. I will admit that it has taken me sometime; I have not fully gotten over it, or reached a point where it makes me 100 percent comfortable.

Chapter 10

"What you see is not always what you get"

He was my knight in shining armor, there during one of the most trying times in my life. He gave me hope and a retreat to a better life. I was still dealing with the trauma from my stalker, but he really got me to come out of my shell. We spent a lot of time together; he reassured me that he understood what I had gone through, and he wanted me just to take my time, relax, and smell the roses. His whole outlook on life was that we only live once, life is too short to get stuck in a place in time so full of negativity. I thought about what he was saying, and slowly I was able to pull myself out of the fear. I began to have a yearning to live life, and be happy.

Our fairytale developed and we spent two years of bliss. He would help me with my shop and the children when he could. He always tried to find a way to put a smile on my face and made me feel safe.

After one and a half years of being together, I got pregnant. Yeah. I was told I couldn't have another child due to having endometriosis and having had multiple surgeries. So, to say it was a surprise was an understatement.

I was so happy. God had given us a baby. He had a child from his previous marriage. So, blending his, mine, and ours was definitely a challenge. Our marriage had hit some bumps in the road, just like any other marriages would, and we just made the necessarily arrangements along the way.

We were married for 13 years and by this time arguments and our tempers were getting worse and a little more, but it wasn't an isolated incident. I think it was a combination of everything. Life, raising children, bringing families together, and work. I was always thinking and wondering and asking myself, *what can I do? What should I do? Did I do something wrong?* I wondered if we were going through more issues since I had gained weight over the years. It did. He did not look at me the same he did years ago. They say, in all marriages, you go through, hit a wall, and you have to find a way to make it better. It was. I was left alone in our relationship to be a solo code caretaker of our son. My husband worked long hours.

Lack of attention became an issue between my husband and me. I noticed a disconnect between us and I tried hard to do what I could do to change our direction, and this relationship I felt was going South fast.

Our marriage ended, and even though we were divorced on paper, we continued our relationship for years. Thinking back, I can remember how excited I once was to ride into work together. Uh, work soon opened my eyes to the lies. My life had become rumors confirming his ongoing relationship with his current wife. I had learned of others before her, some had become dear friends. Others had their guilt behind their smiles, but I knew. And so did he. I had asked him several times through the years, if he was having other relations with other women, his answers were always the same, "No. If I can't make it work with you, I can't make it work with anybody." Then, one day he just disappeared without a word, not even a goodbye, no forwarding address for him or my son. Our son had moved in with him after graduating from high school. Not only did they move, they moved out of the town where we both had lived, which made it easy for both of us to take care of our son. I felt there was no reason to contact him for his actions. He proved he was a liar. Not only was my life partner, my protector, and my friend of 22 years gone, so was my son. As I would take the long drive into work alone, many thoughts would run through my mind. *Why wouldn't he just tell me he was seeing somebody? Why did I have to learn it at work? I wonder who she is. I wonder if I see her. I wonder if he talked about her. As I would walk into work I would pray every day, "God, please do not let me see them together. I'm not ready. I need time for this to process."*

Did the thought cross my mind to get another job? Yes, every single day, but I kept on holding my head up high. I deserved to work there, just as much as they did. People would tell me all the time, "I don't know how you do it. I could never do it." I would just say, "By the grace of God and I pray a lot."

It has been difficult losing my partner on this long journey with our child, who will continue to need guidance and support throughout his entire adult life. I have found a peace I hadn't felt in years. His absence had become the biggest blessing of my life. My knight in shining armor had turned out to be just another bad decision.

Chapter 11
"All My Children"

We are all products of our environment. I have learned over the years that the type of adult you become and the type of parent you become are a sum of all that you have experienced. As a young girl, I went through a lot but I also had a balance of good things that happened in my life. I wonder now which ones outweighed the next. I know that whatever it was I have gone through will show somewhere in my life, either good or bad. That old saying is, "A good tree will bear you only good fruit and a bad tree bears bad fruit." The saying is accurate to a point, because some of the best people can have the worst-acting children. So, I kept all these things in my mind during my relationships and marriages, but mostly, a big question was always lingering in my mind, *Will I be enough?*

The role of a parent is very challenging. You know every little step that you make and everything that you do will ultimately affect your children. I looked back on my relationship with my parents and also my crazy adventure of this thing we call life, and wondered if I could actually do the job. The moment I found out I was pregnant, I was happy and afraid at the same time. I had accepted a role that was going to last a lifetime. I had something of an issue with my personal commitment to things, like finishing what I started. Sometimes, it always sounded like a great idea, but then I would lose interest, but parenthood was something I could not just put away on the shelf and come back to it later. Believe me, I took some time to psych myself up. I thought to myself, *I loved playing with dolls and even babysat from time to time; this should be a piece of cake,* yet the dolls required no food and the babies would go home after a while.

I'm pregnant! Dinner for two. Baby on board. I have something cooking in the oven! I was petrified behind all of my smiles, because this was it, no turning back, this journey into motherhood was finally here and there was no room for errors. *I have to get it right, I have to be, to a little human being, what my mom had been for me as I was growing up, present, caring, loving and attentive.* See, that's where my commitment kicks in, being attentive to another living soul. *Can I dedicate that much time? Am I ready?*

The day came, I was 34 weeks and my son was doing flips and turns, poking his elbow, feet and head against every section of my ribcage; he was ready to make his entrance into the world. I was in labor for no more than two hours before my water broke and he started his way, bullying his way, you would say, into life! Now the pain was out of this world. I needed all the drugs the doctor could give me to help me through pushing my son out of my body and into the world. I could feel him moving around and the pressure pushed back on every organ in my body, so much so that I had the hiccups for an hour afterwards. I pushed and pushed and he finally came out and it felt like a million pounds was lifted off of me, once he made his way out. I couldn't believe it! That beautiful bouncing baby boy was inside of me all this time! Then it hit me. The excitement had settled down and now I was thinking about the rest of our lives, just in that moment. I questioned myself, *What have I done and will I be able to take care of him?* Yes, I had help, but at the end of the day, its Momma's baby daddy's, maybe. I just wanted the best for him and to be all I could be for him, fearing that I never wanted to be a failure in his little eyes. I became so over whelmed that I began to cry, not of happiness but pure terror.

I thought back to my childhood and all of what happened to me, and I swore that I would guard my son and even give my life if I had to, to protect him. Knowing just how cruel this world could be, I knew that I had to give him my all. In return, he gave me all of his love. The love that my son gave me was immeasurable, I never knew love like this before, until my daughter was born.

I would hear the old wives tale about having children, "Once you have one, you gonna want to have another one, especially if the first is a boy, you would want one of each." I guess there was something to it, because I was pregnant again. My children are two years apart. Once I heard I was having a girl, I was head-over-heels in love with the thought, not just of having a girl, but to have two humans who would love me unconditionally. You know how people say that the first baby is the experiment, and you will make a lot of mistakes, but the second one will be the one you apply your learned mistakes to. Well, they actually are considered one in the same. I didn't have time between the two to take notes on what went wrong or right with my babies, so it was trial by fire double time!

My children took away selfishness. Generally speaking, we all have a little selfish way in us. I didn't really know what that was anymore, being selfish or having time to myself; they kept me busy. Being a mother was a full-time job and having multiple children just made it more demanding. I found joy in the job of parenthood. I believe it was my calling and my saving grace.

During the crazy part in my life, I kept my children in the forefront of my mind; at all costs I would protect them. They made me better, they made me an even better parent, knowing that I was moving in a way to keep them at peace. I did my best, but there were still a lot of times that I did not live up to the expectations I put on myself as a mother, role model, and protector. We live and we learn and our hopes is that our children are not forever scared from the situations and things that we chose to do and engage in in life.

"Girl Power," my baby girl put up a fight, I tell you. They say that every pregnancy is different and I learned the hard way that this one would be totally different from the first. She was stubborn, she did not want to come out, it was almost like she found a good, warm spot, and its cold outside, so why would you? I was in labor with her for 17 hours, back and forth, through pain and nausea, Braxton Hicks and all. Finally, she decided to come on out. But she tried to tear me a new one! They had to literally pull her out of me, kicking and screaming. The first sight of her and I could have sworn she frowned at me like, "Hey! I was sleeping there!"

I could share my love with my son and give him affection, but my baby girl was on a whole other level. I envisioned the days that I spent doing my baby doll's hair, playing dress-up, having tea parties, and even remembering the time I did pageants. *Wow, we have a lot to do baby girl!*

We shared a lot of those girlie things that I wanted to do with her and it was pure magic, purple hearts and pink cotton candy. I had my daughter on the 4th of July, and she definitely was my firecracker baby! Even through the worst of times it was all good; I still had them. I paid close attention to their likes and dislikes and the characteristics they both shared with me and their father. So, it was a great balancing act. Those of you who have multiple children know exactly what I am talking about. Having that even love and attention for both children is very crucial to their overall development as children to teens and to young adults. I enjoyed being a mother and just trying to mirror what my mother did for us when we were coming up. I made it my job to be present at all the games, recitals and programs, cheering them on and letting them know just how much their mother loved them. As if it couldn't get any better!

Years later, after remarrying in my 30's, I was once again pregnant, waiting on another bundle of joy to share all my love with and do the best I could to not mess it up. Again you live and you learn through all the relationships and just living life in general we learn.

In life, they say, you will have your challenges and, if you live long enough, you will learn from them and learn how to make lemonade out of lemons. I was well-versed in creating and doing more than just a little bit with those lemons. My next marriage had its challenges and issues, but we tried our best to work through it all. The baby of them all was born during the middle of our winter months, living in a high snow area prone to long winters, and we were smack dab in the middle. The roads were full of snow and the snow drifts were piled up so high they hovered over cars. It was a rough winter, being 40 lbs. heavier about to pop on the coldest day of the year. Baby number three! Third time is the charm, right? In this case, yes, a very easy birth. Now my other two children were well into their post toddler years when their baby brother was born. The oldest children had a good relationship with their father so they would go to spend time with him just about every weekend, and when they didn't, my daughter did a great job in helping me out with their little brother. To have three great children who were respectful, loving and appreciative was, and is, always a blessing. I thought that at least, by just the way life is, I would have one child who would give me a problem, but none of them were ever a problem… knock on wood!

My oldest son:

And my oldest son is my baby Jesus. That's what I call him. He's the kindest and sweetest. If I ever need anything, he's there. He has the best heart I have ever seen in my life and will give you the shirt off of his back.

My daughter:

My daughter's a good person, but she's snappy. She is the most giving person and very hard on herself, being a people-pleaser. She will go out of her way to help anyone. She is very successful as a wife and parent. She is absolutely gorgeous and just as beautiful outside as she is inside. Her smile lights up the room with the most white and beautiful teeth you will ever see.

Baby Boy:

We found out that he had an extra need and flourished with one-on-one attention, and he did not like drama. He was just like any other child at that age, unsure about himself and learning to stay confident. He had some learning issues in school and tried his best to be social. He had a hard time in school, and as he got older, he tried to adjust. I know that my relationship with his father had a lot to do with how he developed. He was his father's son and at times their relationship would get rocky, but they loved each other dearly.

My love for my children kept me from becoming a substance abuser. I smoked some cigarettes but hated weed. I was never a heavy drinker at all. The one thing that I did have, health-wise were bad stomach ulcers from worrying, because that's one thing that I suffered from. I was stressed every single day, and at times sleep was my best friend, when I could get it. So, drinking alcohol was a no-no because my stomach would not allow me to be a heavy drinker. That was a blessing for sure, because I think I might have become a heavy drinker without that particular issue. Most times, you will hear that with the things that I have gone through, it is normal to suppress your issues with alcohol or drugs. I know my children kept me from doing something stupid.

Chapter 12
"Heart of Gold"

All of my life I always wanted children, some one that I could share all of my love with. I knew that children would love me back unconditionally. Even after having children of my own I always showed love to other people's children also, because I had plenty of love to give. I am now divorced for the second time and have learned more about myself after this last marriage. My heart is very big and I give everyone the benefit of the doubt. Wearing my heart on my sleeve has left me disillusioned and heartbroken, but nothing could be further from the truth. I still believe in love, caring for others and trusting other people to do unto me as I have done for them.

I am a big cry baby and a purist at heart. I love to see others laugh, smile, and enjoy their life, and sharing love unconditionally with them has always been my thing.

My children have always had a way of making friends and keeping good relationships with them. I would attribute that to how I raised them. Most times it's not what you say but what you do that children pay attention to, and that is the truth. If they see you as the parent doing bad things, naturally they will have bad habits and be terrible people. My next chapter in life gave me so much fulfillment and I know it helped my children to become more well-rounded adults.

I became a foster parent of four children, Marie 8, and three siblings, Joshua 5, Kelly, and Tameka 8. Kelly was the 11-month-old, who needed a loving home and a parent who could share love and take good care of them. I was a blessing and also an adventure that I would share with these precious little souls. Most of them hadn't done some of the most common things in life or even seen or heard of most things, partly because of their circumstances, so it made for quite an eye-opening time. The experience was an overall good one; the children learned from one another and I learned a lot from them, also.

Here is the makeup of my little precious angels; three girls, one white and the others black, and one boy that was black. I often wondered if this was gonna be something that would be difficult for me because of the cultural differences, but I soon learned that all a child ever needs is love, discipline and a good, caring mother, and everything would work itself out.

Being that we all were in the same boat, having the first of something in common, I took my time to get to know the children. I know that it can be a challenge and hard to get to know a child, especially when the circumstances are of a wide range, some escaping abuse, some having no father or mother, the mother being on drugs, and in limbo in foster care until someone chooses them. I thought that the approach that I took with my own children would be the best offense and defense. My first introduction to the little boy went a little something like this;

I'm sitting at home in the shop. I had gotten off the phone with the state just about an hour and I was expecting the child to be dropped off any minute now. I never heard the car come and go, then I heard a couple of knocks, which sounded like acorns dropping on the sidewalk from the trees out front, so I didn't quite pay it any mind. The next sounds I heard were Bang! Bang! Bang! Against the side of the house, which really got my attention. I ran to the shop door and looked around the corner. I saw a figure, then on closer inspection from up under a hat which was two sizes too big, a baggie over coat, baggie pants held up by a belt three sizes too big, a little arm is rearing back about to throw another rock up against my house. I screamed out,

"Hey!"

He was already in full swing, so my yell did not manage to stop his follow through. Bang! The rock hit my house with the force of a baseball thrown by Nolan Ryan! It hit hard! He went back into the dirt searching for the next rock as I started to pick up the pace walking towards him to stop the next assault on my house.

He looked up at me as I got closer and just stared. We both just stared at each other, then I was confused. I looked around and did not see a car or anyone else around. I thought the agency said that they would come in and complete the paperwork and introduce me to my new foster child, but no one was there.

I introduced myself to him and told him with a stern voice, "If you throw one rock, I'm gonna make you build me another beauty shop with them!"

With a grin, he acknowledged my threat and reached out his hand and told me his name. I could see that he had a little bag behind him, filled with his only possessions. I assured him he was in the right place and had nothing to worry about, we would be good friends. He stood there with his bag behind him and just stared. After a couple minutes of small talk he felt comfortable enough to come inside, so I gave him a tour of the house and shop. He really loved watching TV and he sat down and ate lunch while glued to the TV.

That day was a special day because I was getting my Fab 4 and they were being released or brought to me from different agents, which made the process nerve-wracking. Believe me, I had some choice words for the other agency or person who just left him out there by himself. By day's end, we were all together.

Each child had experienced some type of trauma and it was a forever growing storyline narrated by one of my sweet and precious babies. You can not imagine what their little ears would hear, little eyes would see, and little bodies have to endure; it was heart breaking. All I wanted to do was to shower them with love and make sure they had a place they could call home and escape the terror until the agency, state, or even a responsible family member could come and get them.

My Joshua had separation anxiety and he was not a fan of hugs, kisses or even the slightest bit of touch. He was a bed-wetter, he had his own room, at my house and was embarrassed when he wet the bed. I made sure that the other kids did not know that he wet the bed, so the plan was to recover the sheets and clothes and have his stuff ready for him when he woke up. He would wake up, come downstairs, take that dirty underwear and put it in the bag, and wash them when the girls were upstairs in the restroom. We just washed it and they never knew; he was tickled to death about that, because before he would get teased about wetting the bed. Now no one could tease him and it became our little secret until he stopped wetting the bed.

One of my oldest, Tamekia, when she was just getting acquainted with the house, I allowed them to walk around. Each child had a bag with them with their possessions in them and I mentioned to them that they could leave their bags downstairs and walk around upstairs. While introducing all the children, they were amazed at the shop, especially the girls. They just livened up, but none of them had anything to say; they were quiet. On our way up-stairs, I smelled something that took my breath away. After getting all the children settled, I spoke to the oldest and asked her if I could see her bag. There was poop in her bag. I had to clean out the bag and we had to get her new clothes. After sitting her down and asking her about what was going on, she asked me for another bag, so she could use it for the bathroom when she needed to go to the bathroom. Learning this broke my heart. She was going to the bathroom in a bag which she kept it in her bookbag after she was done. After we got everything cleaned and thrown away, she kept asking me for another bag and it took a while to get her to use the regular bathroom. I can only imagine that type of hell she was going through before she got to me.

When our newest member showed up, Tamekia went out to the car with a baby doll to welcome her and spoke to her to reassure her, "Don't cry, don't worry, we live with an angel, you will be alright." Marie cried for two to three nights straight and was afraid of the dark. I would have to leave the lights on when they went to bed and they needed me to hold their hands while they slept. I would lay at the bottom of the bed each night until they both went to sleep. They had little to no trust with anyone, male or female. It took a while to help them all with their particular issues and I was more than prepared to help them.

Joshua had a thing for rocks, so I would take him down to the lake and he could throw all the rocks he wanted out into the lake until he got tired. The girls finally started coming around to learn how to do hair; they really enjoyed watching me do hair.

The best times we all had was during dinnertime, when each child would clean their plate; I mean nothing was left! We had grown together as a family. They got to experience what it was like to have a family and I learned just how bad each one of them had it, and it was heartbreaking. If I could have adopted them, I would have, but I was a temporary stay for them. I made sure I let the agency and state know that I needed them to end up in the best place for them. My Fab 4 were easy to take care of because they had nothing, and everything I did for them was so appreciated.

The children played like there was no tomorrow, fully acclimated to their new home. We would learn from each other. I learned I had some smart children on my hands and very athletic, also. I remember setting up obstacle courses in the backyard and watching them run. Tamekia could run like the wind and could climb like nobody's business. Joshua had perfect balance and Marie had great stamina and could play all day long.

Dinnertime was the time they would decompress and start sharing all the things they had experienced. I tell you, some nights I would sit up and cry, wondering how someone could be so cruel to a defenseless child.

The baby, Kelly, when she was getting quiet, she'd sleep a lot. I mean, she was sleeping 12, 13, 14 hours. So, I let her do that two or three days before I called the social worker. She was sleeping too long and they could suspend you sometimes when nobody cared. I took her to the doctors and they told me it was normal that a baby coming out of a bad situation would sleep. And they said what they'd was just lay there, and I broke my heart. So, she started walking. She gained five pounds, she was dancing and singing, and it was one of the best times of my life. My daughter was my saving grace; she would watch the children when she had time. She was a college student at the time and helped out until I found daycare for them.

Joshua had taken a liking to lighters and played with them. He had burned down his mother's house. The other children shared stories of abuse and neglect. They all wanted to be with family, and the family that they had left were either grandparents.

I had them for five months. Joshua went to live with his dad's mom. Kelly was adopted by a good family that was close by. Tamekia went back to stay with her grandmother, and Marie went back with her mom. I loved my time with my Fab 4 and I pray everyday that they are growing up healthy and happy.

My son and Sunny were really good friends; he came over from India and he came to church with my son. They got an apartment together and he had become another son of mine. He lived with me for two years and we did what a mother would do for their child when there are cultural differences in washing properly and even deodorant, so I had to teach him how to take care of his hygiene. He is considered one of my children and I talk to him just about every day. He had gone through a lot of things with his family. He was here trying to work and survive and was put in jail for not being here legally. ICE came and got him and we were able to get him back and help save his life.

Sunny struggled with substance abuse and drinking; he lives with a church family now and has dealt with so much discrimination and we have been through hell and back with him.

To this day, I consider myself as having had 8 children! I have been forever changed having the experiences with my bonus children. Life never seems to stop amazing me with the challenges we all have faced together. My heart will always be with them and theirs are surely with mine.

Chapter 13
"Why does everyone
Hate Cyndi?"

I ask myself sometimes, *"Why?" I have been a good friend, daughter, partner, wife and mother.* Don't get the chapter title wrong at all, I just wondered. Without exception, my children have loved me through thick and thin, and have not had anything to say about me in a negative light. That has not been true of everyone I've known, or who has known me. I have learned that sometimes the hate is not really hating, it is a feeling of disgust for what I may have been doing in life or whom I was dealing with in life, but even then, that was taken out of context.

I have had some rough moments in life and other moments that have left me so hurt that I questioned again, "Why?" I have gone into detail in this book about some things, and others I have chosen not to go into detail at all, because it has hurt me so much that it is very hard to speak on. Yes, there is so much more, but I will leave it up to your imagination. And for those who have not believed in me at those moments in time, trust me, I gave you no reason to judge me.

This has been one of the best and worst experiences of retelling stories of my life, coming face-to-face with some truths that I thought I would never relive again. I was told before that I should tell the truth and shame the devil, tell the truth, the whole truth, so help me God. It's good to let out all of it, but some truth is just too real to be revealed. The wounds run real deep, so now I can deal with them in private. I have allowed you who have read this book about my life to

71

get a glimpse of it and get a better understanding of me. Those stories that went untold really have shaped my life, and even though there are plenty more untold stories, these will have to be enough for now. I had to take a step back and look at the bigger picture when looking into telling the story of my life and other stories that made me who I am today. A lot of times, people look at you for face value and truly have no clue just what has happened to you.

Sometimes it's your family who misjudge your character; they fall victim to believing someone else over you, and that has to be the most hurtful feeling ever. Why would you believe someone else and not me? Why would you try to sweep something under the rug and act like it did not happen? I know that certain things are very hard to face or even relive, but these things could haunt a person for a lifetime and keep them in a mode of silence that will lead them down the wrong road time and time again. I have realized that certain situations in life required me to have a voice, be loud, aggressive, and assertive, to be heard; it never came because it was shut down years prior. It took me some time to analyze my life and all my actions, what kind of person I had become, the victim, battered wife, emotional dumping ground, timid and quiet friend.

Living in fear keeps you from truly living at all; you just go day-by-day existing. We reject the one thing that will set us free because we don't feel worthy of owning it, and that's our voice. We question ourselves daily, "Why" and when I say "we," I'm saying all women who have gone through similar things that I have gone through and have lost their way and their voices because of the fear. Fear gets passed down. You can stifle yourself and others with your mindset, being too conservative, not venturing outside of the box that was built for you, it handicaps you.

I decided to take this journey, go back down memory lane, face my fears and answer my own question, "Why?" I have been set free from all that held me down. You know, words are very powerful, they can shape the minds and hearts of children, mold and control the bodies of vulnerable women, turn those who love you against you in a heartbeat. What connection do we have with the words that control and move our lives in different directions? If you don't know the answer to that question, I will tell you now. You have all the control. You are connected to the words that you speak, and the words you allow to define you. Choose those words wisely!

I am now breaking out of my shell, breaking out of the usual, what you are comfortable seeing me be, ohh that's Cyndi. No! This is Cyndi. I am Cyndi and with what I have overcome in my lifetime I can write several books. I am no longer a captive of a person, place or thing, I am free to tell my story as I see fit.

If you have gotten this far, I want to say thank you for taking the time to peek into my life, yes, peek. You understand that unpackaging the whole story was a great trial for me and my family. I made sure not to offend anyone in the process but I had to tell the story and release myself from the shame and hurt. I've heard people ask me "Why?" Why would I write about something so personal, so I had to break down my "Whys" and what drove me to expressing my story in this way.

You know that my parents and children mean the world to me and this is the way I honor them by stepping out and doing something that most people could only dream of, have courage and writing a book, face all of my demons, tell the truths that were hidden, show the other side of me, and through it all, show YOU the reader that you too can be UNBEATEN!

www.ingramcontent.com/pod-product-compliance
Lightning Source LLC
Chambersburg PA
CBHW030338020726
47493CB00004B/1327